MY FRIEND

MEi JiNg

TEXT BY
ANNA McQUINN

ARTWORK BY
BEN FREY

PHOTOGRAPHY BY
IRVIN CHEUNG

annick press
toronto + new york + vancouver

My friend is Chinese. Well, actually, she was born here, just like me.

The first day of school, the teacher sat me next to her. She was super nice and loaned me her best pen. We've been friends ever since. My name is Monifa, her name is Mei Jing.

We're in second grade now, and still in the same class.
Our favorite subject is arts and crafts.

Mei Jing and I even have the same favorite color—it's purple. Except sometimes I like pink also.

At Mei Jing's house, we mostly draw lots of pictures. I have glitter pens and she has gel pens and all kinds of felt markers.

When Mei Jing's grandma is there, which is a lot, she doesn't mind too much if we make a mess. She didn't even get mad when some glitter got mushed into the white carpet.

华峰超级市场

所鲜蔬菜

Mei Jing calls her grandma Paw Paw. Her grandma calls her Mui Mui—which means "little girl" in Cantonese. But Mei Jing is her proper name. Mei means "beautiful" and Jing means "sparkling crystal."

My name means "I am lucky" in Yoruba, which is a language they speak in Nigeria. Mei Jing's grandma says it's the best name ever.

At my house, we mostly play dressing up. Sometimes I'm Queen Sophia, Tatiana, Katerina the First, and Mei Jing is Queen Priscilla, Victoria, Elegantina.

Our secret palace is under the stairs and we take turns sitting on the throne.

One day I went with Mei Jing to her grandma's house. Mei Jing's aunts and cousins were there—what a lot of people!

I thought it must be someone's birthday, but Mei Jing says her whole family gets together all the time. Everyone spent all afternoon eating and talking. Mei Jing's dad showed me how to use chopsticks.

I tried lots of things I'd never tasted before. Best of all I liked the fish balls, but everything was good. Mei Jing told me I was lucky her grandma hadn't cooked chicken feet!

My gramma likes weird stuff too. She says that when she was a girl, her favorite thing to eat was cow's foot. Yuck!

Mei Jing's grandma came here from Hong Kong when she was only six.

Her mom and dad started a restaurant and worked hard all day and night. Sometimes Mei Jing's grandma had to help too, even though she was so little. Mei Jing's grandma says you have to work hard to start a new life.

In March, Mei Jing got a new puppy. He's so cute. We thought up lots of names, but we decided Patches was best because of his dark spots.

Every time we take Patches to the park, he just wants to run, run, run.

Mei Jing and I are going to be veterinarians when we're big. We're going to have a huge clinic. Animals can come if they are sick or just to get a treat.

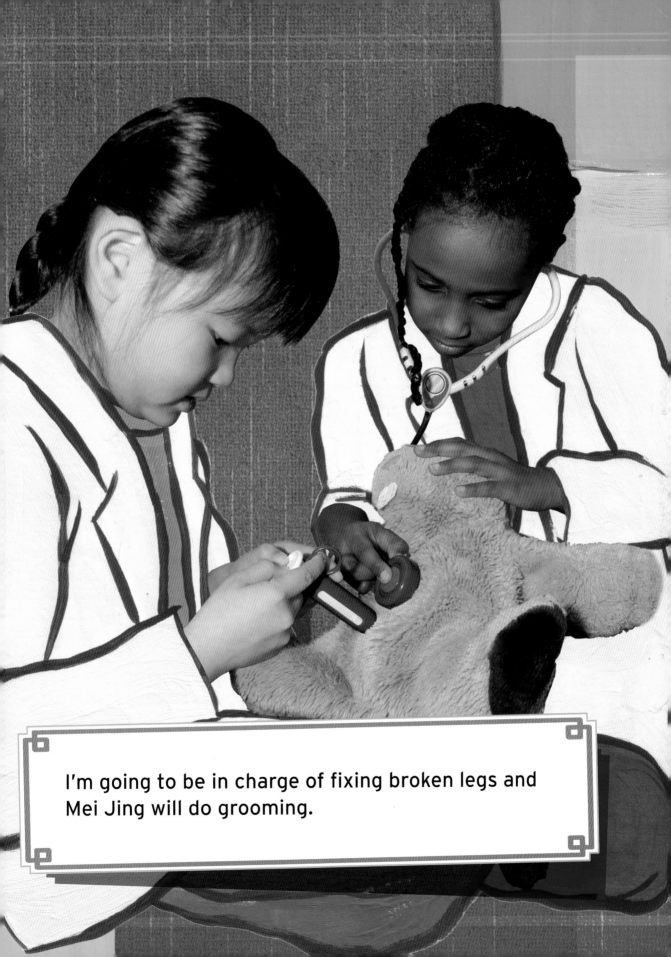

I'm going to be in charge of fixing broken legs and Mei Jing will do grooming.

Mei Jing and I go to drama club on Tuesdays. For Chinese New Year, we all learned the Dragon Dance.

Then we put on a show at the community center.
Mei Jing and I started laughing and couldn't stop,
right in the middle of it! But no one seemed to mind.

After, Mei Jing's parents gave Mei Jing and me red envelopes for a new year's gift. We made red envelopes in school, but they only had chocolate coins inside. Mei Jing's family put in real money!

Mei Jing says she also gets them on her birthday and when she gets good grades, so I bet she will be rich soon.

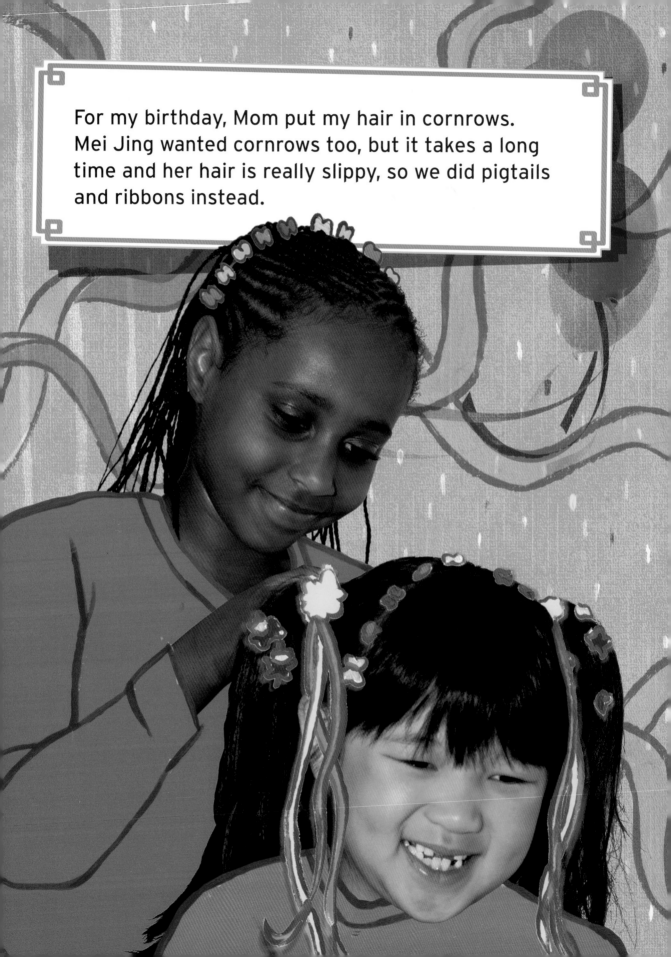

For my birthday, Mom put my hair in cornrows. Mei Jing wanted cornrows too, but it takes a long time and her hair is really slippy, so we did pigtails and ribbons instead.

Mei Jing gave me a pretty charm bracelet—it has flowers inside glass beads and hearts and butterflies. It also has a little Chinese coin.

Later on, we went to play in the backyard, and saw my mom's big African blanket hanging on the line. So we decided to make it into a tent.

We even pretended to roast marshmallows—
I ate the pink ones and Mei Jing ate the white ones.

On Saturdays, we usually go to the playground.
Mei Jing can get higher than me on the swings, but
mostly we try to match each other. That's because
we're best friends.

The photographer would like to thank Victoria Cheung and Martha Asfaw and their families for their invaluable contribution.

The author would like to thank Sho Ying and Amy for all their help, and Katie, Isabel, Sebastian and Isabella for being inspiring.

This book is dedicated to My Friends—Margaret, Jana, Marijn and Susanna who all know how to really listen . . .

Annick Press Ltd.
Main photos (Monifa, Mei Jing, and family) by Irvin Cheung. Artwork by Ben Frey. Additional photography credits: playground: © istockphoto.com/Rami Ben Ami; single house: © istockphoto.com/Jim Pruitt; row of houses: © istockphoto.com/Oktay Ortakcioglu; deciduous tree: © istockphoto.com/Christine Balderas; coniferous tree: © istockphoto.com/Olga Zinatova; pottery tools: ©istockphoto.com/Jason Lugo; lump of clay: © Irvin Cheung; vase: © istockphoto.com/Coral Coolahan; dresser: © istockphoto.com; potted plant: © istockphoto.com/Eliza Snow; bok choy, choy sum, cordyceps fungi: © istockphoto.com/Norman Chan; lychee: © istockphoto.com/John Peacock; durian: © istockphoto.com/Fadhil Kamarudin; red Chinese lanterns: © istockphoto.com/Frank van den Bergh; hanging lamps: © Irvin Cheung; lantern fruit and cinnamon sticks: © istockphoto.com/Junghee Choi; stair railing: © istockphoto.com/Nina Shannon; vacuum cleaner: © istockphoto.com/Emrah Turudu; leather trunk: © istockphoto.com/Les Palenik; suitcase: © istockphoto.com; cardboard boxes: © istockphoto.com/Carlos Alvarez; castle: © istockphoto.com; butterfly (right and left): © istockphoto.com/Cathy Keifer; butterfly (center) © istockphoto.com/Goran Kapor; brick houses: © istockphoto.com/Owen Price; flower pattern texture: © istockphoto.com/senkonate; plates of food: © Irvin Cheung; chicken's foot: © istockphoto.com/Sawayasu Tsuji; cow's hoof: © istockphoto.com/Jorge Gonzalez; Hong Kong ferry: © istockphoto.com/Tan Kian Khoon; Hong Kong tram: © Christine Gonslaves/Dreamstime.com; Jade Palace restaurant, Calgary, Alberta: Glenbow Archives NA-2645-53; family portrait, restaurant interior: Courtesy of Ken Chow; photo album: © istockphoto.com; envelope: © istockphoto.com/Anja Hild; wood texture: © istockphoto.com/Bill Noll; Jack Russell terrier: © istockphoto.com/Claudio Arnese; pagoda and trees: © istockphoto.com; picture frame: © istockphoto.com/Csaba Zsarnowszky; clock: © istockphoto.com; thermometer: © istockphoto.com/Eugene Berman; bandages: © istockphoto.com/Yunus Arakon; black dart and blue dart: © istockphoto.com; red dart: © istockphoto.com/Boris Yankov; green pennant: © istockphoto.com/Stefan Klein; red checkered pennant: © istockphoto.com/Valerie Loiseleux; chest of coins: © istockphoto.com/Ivan Mateev; diamonds: © istockphoto.com/Evgeny Terentyev; pile of gold coins: © istockphoto.com/Elnur Amikishiyev; stack of bills and piggy banks: © istockphoto.com/Ivana Starcevic; balloons: © istockphoto.com; glass heart: © istockphoto.com/Liudmila Otrutskaya; cloisonné eggs: © istockphoto.com/Hector Joseph Lumang; blue glass bead and butterfly bead: © istockphoto.com; Chinese coin: © istockphoto.com/Hector Joseph Lumang; clothes-peg: © istockphoto.com/Patricia Nelson; African blanket pattern: © istockphoto.com/Peeter Viisimaa; kerosene lantern: © istockphoto.com/Juan Monino; Calgary skyline: © istockphoto.com; gerbera daisies: © istockphoto.com/Kais Tolmats

Edited by Pam Robertson
Copyedited by Elizabeth McLean
Proofread by Helen Godolphin
Cover and interior design by Irvin Cheung / iCheung Design, inc.

We acknowledge the support of the Canada Council for the Arts, the Ontario Arts Council, and the Government of Canada through the Book Publishing Industry Development Program (BPIDP) for our publishing activities.

Cataloging in Publication
McQuinn, Anna
    My friend Mei Jing / text by Anna McQuinn ; artwork by Ben Frey ; photography by Irvin Cheung.

(My friend— series)
ISBN 978-1-55451-153-2 (bound).–ISBN 978-1-55451-152-5 (pbk.)

    I. Frey, Ben, 1978– II. Cheung, Irvin III. Title. IV. Series.
PZ7.M247Mym 2009   j823'.92   C2008-905908-5

Printed and bound in China

Published in the U.S.A. by
Annick Press (U.S.) Ltd.

Distributed in Canada by
Firefly Books Ltd.
66 Leek Crescent
Richmond Hill, ON
L4B 1H1

Distributed in the U.S.A. by
Firefly Books (U.S.) Inc.
P.O. Box 1338
Ellicott Station
Buffalo, NY 14205

Visit our website at **www.annickpress.com**